Martha Agnes Rand

The Legend of a Thought, and Other Verses

Martha Agnes Rand

The Legend of a Thought, and Other Verses

ISBN/EAN: 9783337393526

Printed in Europe, USA, Canada, Australia, Japan

Cover: Foto ©Andreas Hilbeck / pixelio.de

More available books at **www.hansebooks.com**

THE

LEGEND OF A THOUGHT

AND

OTHER VERSES.

BY

MARTHA AGNES RAND.

———————

CHICAGO, 1889

CONTENTS.

TO MY FATHER.

Happy those days of sojourn and of rest,
   When foreign lands allured my venturous feet;
Of all to me one valley was the best,
   And yet my summer there was incomplete,
Because I missed one far across the sea—
   Who once had led me, as a little child,
Through those same woodland paths, and looked
        with me
   On those same mountain ranges, near and wild.
He showed me where the soulful gentian dwelt,
   And broke for me the rose's thorny stem,
And loved the graceful flowers, because he felt
   And loved the unseen hand that fashioned them.
And so there came to me an idle whim
   That I would pluck stray flowers, from time to time,
Along thought's road, that I might take to him
   A little nosegay from the realms of rhyme.
And if my flowers prove but homely weeds
   From out a soil of immaturity,
Still he, I know, will pardon as he reads,
   And love them, for the love they bear from me.

THE LEGEND OF A THOUGHT.

I.

Once, long ago, in a glassy stream,
   Where never a ripple wrought,
With the pictured flush of the morning's gleam,
And the azure sky and the sun's soft beam,
   There was mirrored a human thought.

It had taken the form of a fragile bird,
   Of all God's living things ;
Pure white it looked; but, as it stirred,
It could be seen the little bird
   Had dark spots on its wings.

For not all pure as snowflake white
   That thought, not free from stain;
Yet eagerly it sought the right,
Aspired to know truth's purest light,
   Deep wisdom to attain.

High, high it soared, and higher still,
   From morning's dawn till even,
And earth grew dim and space grew chill,
Yet on it soared, nor paused until
   It reached the gates of Heaven.

There long without it strove to bide,
  One little glimpse to win
Of what the golden gates denied
(For Heaven's gates were high and wide),
  It could not see within.

At length, despairing of the things
  For which it long had striven,
It ceased its vain imaginings,
And beat its little tired wings
  Against the gates of Heaven.

II.

Before Jehovah's presence brought
  The white-robed heavenly host
Their festal offerings, and sought
Which of the gifts their love had wrought
  Might please the Father most.

Fair tokens laid they at his feet,
  So rich, so passing rare,
No mortal eye their forms may meet,
And flowers of such a perfume sweet
  As wafts but heavenly air.

Then, as with song and sacred rite
  They praised Jehovah's name,

With one accord they cast their sight
Adown the path of shining light
　　Where, lo, the Christ child came!

A gift he bore, a burden sweet,
　　Held closely to his breast,
While now and then the baby feet
Stood halting, then with trust complete
　　Again they forward pressed.

Before his Lord, with troubled smile,
　　He paused, as fearful still
The snow-white altar to defile,
And lisped, half falteringly the while,
　　As little children will—

"Dear Lord, 't is but a wayward thing,
　　An earthly gift. I know,
But I found it sadly hovering
Without the gates, and I let it in—
　　Because—I loved it so."

Then forward all the angels pressed:
　　No faintest sound was heard
As from its safe and cozy nest
Within the little Christ-child's breast
　　There fluttered forth a bird !

Straight from the baby arms it flew
  Towards the Father's throne;
Then nearer still the angels drew,
While breathless wondered they anew,
  And gazed where it had flown.

For, strain their vision as they would,
  Of birdling there was nought:
But in its place a dazzling flood
Of light, within whose radiance stood
  Revealed the human Thought.

And soft upon the evening air,
  Like music sweet and near,
Like music sweet beyond compare,
In words replete with accent rare,
  A voice fell low and clear—

"Oh, best of all, thou Son of mine,
  This token thou hast given!
For half of earth and half divine,
It is this very gift of thine
  Shall link the world with Heaven."

THE TENEMENT BABY.

The sea breeze swept o'er the pleasant beach,
  And fondled the golden curls
Of rich-born children, and kissed them each,
  And romped with the boys and girls.

But its breath reached not the stifling room
  On a narrow alley way,
Where, feebly struggling against its doom,
  A poor, sick baby lay.

The little features were pinched and white;
  And, oh, so weak, and thin
The tiny form, so sad the blight
  Of the restless life within!

The mother's courage was well nigh spent—
  A kind physician said:
"You need more sleep, more nourishment."
  But the woman shook her head—

"There's little sleep ever comes this way,
  For the crowd, and the talking wild,
And I've earned no crust since yesterday,
  And I have no food for my child.

"And it's air he needs! Fresh air! Oh, sir!
    Last night I dreamed I took
My baby where the pine and fir
    Made sweet a sea-coast nook.

"The starving lungs breathed in God's free,
    Pure air; the pale cheek flushed,
And he smiled so sweetly up at me!
    And I woke—and the foul air rushed

"Through the door ajar, and I softly crept
    To my little one, and there
So white he lay! and, oh, I wept
    For my dream of the salt sea-air!"

And the tired, heartsick woman sighed,
    In her helpless motherhood;
And the doctor left her tearful-eyed.
    He had said the best he could.

And baby? The baby had a ride.
    One sultry August day
A stranger. driving a wagon, cried
    Aloud, as he passed that way:

"I'll give your baby a drive, my frail,
    Worn mother!" So baby went,
  Along with the other children pale,
    From the festering tenement.

  The road they took crossed the cool, green down,
    All sweet with the clover's breath;
  But it led to a grave-yard out of town,
    And the stranger who drove was Death.

IN BERLIN.

The March wind hurries from the seas
And beats about the Linden trees
That shudder in the sunless air.
But still they gather, gather there
Before the palace, young and old,
Nor heed the dampness and the cold.
For 'tis the hour when strangers meet,
And Kaiser Wilhelm comes to greet
The people.   But the time grows late;
'Tis past the hour; the people wait.

They wait, and they have waited long
And restlessly—a motley throng.
Some, citizens who love to come
Again and yet again; and some,
From hilly regions of the Rhine,
Have left their stores of famous wine,
To view the wonders of the town.
There stands a Tyrol peasant brown;
One knows him by his feathered hat.
Yon English tourist turns to chat,
In broken Deutsch the best he can.

And finds a fellow-countryman,
While yonder Austrian soldier spies
A Spanish doña's languid eyes;
And there, all eagerness and awe,
Prepared to launch his shrill "hurrah!"
Perched on paternal shoulders, proud,
And high above the waiting crowd,
Sits young America—for he,
Whate'er his rank, has come to see.
Yes, frowning tramps may shake their fists,
But anarchists, and monarchists,
And staunch republicans, will vie
To have a peep at royalty.

The troops have passed, the music dies
In faint and fainter strains.   All eyes
Are upward turned to that one mark,
The corner palace window.   Hark!
A cheer rings out upon the air,
And see him, he is standing there!
One glimpse the parted curtains show
Of form erect and head of snow;
One moment we behold him stand
And smile, and wave his courtly hand,
And it is over, and the crowd,

Some whispering, some chatting loud,
In scattered groups has gone its way.
"What kindly eyes!" the people say,
And many thoughtful persons add:
"How old he looked, how old and sad!"

The morrow brought another throng
That waited patiently and long,
And, disappointed, turned away—
They did not see his face that day.

What mean this quiet in the air,
These sombre drapings everywhere,
Such solemn looks, without, within?
What grief has come? What ails Berlin?
The Lindens, wound in weeds of woe,
Wave leafless branches to and fro;
Dense human masses surging come
From Brandenburgher Thor to Dome;
From Dome to Brandenburgher Thor
Wells upward, like the ocean's roar,
The hum of myriad voices. See,
The crowd is still, for suddenly

Adown the Lindens marching comes,
To tempo weird and muffled drums,
A vast procession. Ah, I know

The meaning now—that lying low
In mutest, vainest majesty,
'Neath yonder gilded canopy,
With pulseless hands and sightless eyes,
Asleep in death an emperor lies!
And kings and princes walk behind,
And dirges lade the bleak, March wind.
And from the masses gathered there
Floats upward this their silent prayer,
As Hope from Sorrow's self were bred:
"Oh, God in Heaven, bless our *dead*—
God save our *living* emperor!"
For there is one whose heart is sore,
One all too weak, too worn with pain,
To follow in the funeral train.
A grieving son bows low his head,
A loving son—" God bless our dead—
God save our living Emperor;
God bless the dead for evermore!"
And so the vast procession moves
With the dear, silent form it loves,
With measured steps, and rich display
Of woe. Ah, vainly let them lay
That form in stately pomp apart.
His real tomb is a nation's heart.

Berlin has doffed her garments black,
And spring has decked the Linden track
In fair, green colors. But a breeze
Comes whispering to the Linden trees.
And bids them note the sombre cloud
Above—breathes of a waiting shroud,
Of hope, and prayer, and science vain,
And weeds that they shall wear again.
And lo, the cloud descends, like doom,
And bathes the city in its gloom —
Within another palace gate
A second emperor lies in state.
And as the mourners haunt the place
To view the well-belovéd face,
They marvel at divine intent,
That one whose whole life has been spent
In preparation for a crown,
In manhood's prime must lay it down.
Oh, be ye silent, love God's way,
Nor marvel, mourners, for to-day
A text is sent you from on high.
Then heed the silent homily,
And see, in this dear human dust,
God's trial of a nation's trust.

IN MARIENBAD.

AFTER AN OPEN-AIR CONCERT.

The last notes died upon the fragrant air,
  And from the benches rose each woodland guest,
While strolling couples turned, some here, some there,
  To stroll again, away from all the rest.

The harmony had tuned my soul to peace.
  Alone I wandered down a shady way;
Above me bits of blue and sailing fleece,
  And at my feet the smooth pine needles lay.

In old Bohemia cross and shrine abound
  Along the roads, and dot the country way,
While faded wreaths and tokens placed around
  Speak simple faith that questions not to pray.

There in the morning, on his way to care,
  The peasant tells his beads, or evening sees
Some tired woman rest her basket there;
  And in my walk I came on one of these.

'Twas in a little clearing of the pines,
  There, decked with spring's first flowers, and hung
    with charms,
A high-built niche an image quaint enshrines:—
  The Virgin with the Christ-child in her arms.

Alone I stood there, gazing thoughtfully.
  No, not alone—a swallow hopped before;
Its wing seemed hurt; it tried in vain to fly,
  Yet feared my strange intrusion more and more.

Poor little feathered thing! I would have found
  Its trouble, tried to help the little bird,
Have raised it tenderly from off the ground;
  Yet, heedless of my sympathy, it stirred

Its wings and rose, but fell to earth again ;
  Then, with a final effort, high in air
It fluttered straight towards the flower-decked fane
  Above me—and I left it nestled there!

Oh wounded hearts that grope along life's way,
  Oh grieving hearts, go heed the lesson taught!
Raise your poor fluttering wings and seek to-day
  The sacred refuge that the swallow sought.

THE JESTER.

Wild waxed the music, late the ball.
A stranger entered the dazzling hall,
A jester quaint with bells and rhyme,
Stept to life from the olden time.
   And the crowd was still,
While his words went forth: " If any here
Have a wish, let him breathe it in mine ear.
The greatest wish of his secret heart
I am here to grant. Then come, impart
   Your inmost will."

The dancers flocked to gain his ear,
Each with a wish defined and clear—
And oh, what tales to him revealed!
What care those lightsome smiles concealed!
   What boons they craved—
The canceling of debts; defeat
Of rivals; drafts enticing, sweet,
From Lethe's waters ; mystery
Unveiled; and hope of liberty
   For souls enslaved.

Some women begged for screens to hide
Deceit ; some, pale and haggard-eyed,
For beauty they had lost with youth;
Some, heart-sick, craved the light of Truth;
    And lovers sought
Fulfillment of their cherished plans,
Returns to favor, marriage-bans.
But one sat, feeble, old, and white;
They wondered he had come that night—
    Could *he* wish aught ?

For he had boundless wealth, and fame,
And power to wield, and pride of name.
Yet what are all these things at last
When life grows dim? The jester passed,
    With dance and fife.
The old man clutched him eagerly:
" Oh, give me lease of life!" said he,
" Life, and the girl, my promised bride;
    Oh, life to linger at her side!
    Oh, give me *life!*"

A fair girl stood in the brilliant hall.
She seemed the gayest of them all ;

The first to waltz, the last to tire,
But her laugh rang false, though her eyes flashed fire.
    Beneath his breath
The jester said: "Oh, speak your thought—
Or have you naught to wish for, naught,
No precious gem, no love to wed?
Come, what shall't be, young Goldenhead?"
    She whispered: "*Death!*"

THE SPIRIT'S FAREWELL.

Although for many hours the drizzling morn
Hath broken o'er the earth in tears forlorn,
Now have I first awakened to its gloom
And seek to trace faint outlines in the room.—
Why these half-burning tapers here, and why
This solemn loneliness that haunts the eye?
The place, the objects, all are old to me,
And yet with stranger-eyes I seem to see.
Dull memory! I tax thee all in vain;
Thou seem'st in deepest stupor to have lain,
As I, of yesterday oblivious quite,
Down Lethe's stream had floated overnight.

But now, as in a dim recess I peer,
The sinking taper-lights reveal a bier.
Above it bent on friendly forms I gaze
That have surrounded me since childhood's days.
They weep, and linger fondly o'er the sleeper,
And roses place, and twine the ivy-creeper
And smilax fresh about the pillowed head,
While all the air keeps silence for the dead—

Save where the ticking clock-wheel goes its rounds,
And save where, through the open casement, sounds
The patter, patter, of the rain descending
Upon the clammy earth without, weird-blending
With footsteps hushed and whispered words within—
And melancholy lives in all the scene.

Now one by one pass out the silent crowd
Beneath the curtained door, their heads low-bowed,
Slowly and ponderingly, one by one,
Until the last dumb, stricken face has gone.
Faint on the air dies the last muffled tread,
And I am left alone to guard the dead.
Yet nearer let me draw my noiseless feet,
And gently raise the ghastly winding-sheet
That shrouds this luckless form.
                          But what comes o'er me?
A most familiar figure lies before me.
Oh, where can I have seen such kindred face?
In my bewilderment I dare not trace,
For, though the lids are closed above the eyes,
I seem to know the look that underlies,
And could they open!—ah, but now I feel
That naught has ever ope'd them, save my will.
Ah, I do know thee well, old comrade, now,
Though senseless clay ignore my voice—'tis thou

I once have called myself! And, now I see
Death's hand hath fallen, and parted thee and me.
This means the awful, solemn, silent spell,
And I am here to breathe thee my farewell.
Oh, who that tyrant force shall understand
That frees and dooms to waste, with smiting hand?
Around me others saw I, 'neath the stroke,
Forsake the clinging pressure of thy yoke.
Yet never ventured I to think of *thee*
As sleeping through the vast eternity;
Ne'er fancied this cold dew upon *thy* brow.
And these poor folded hands so quiet now,
But yesterday it was I saw them moved
To active measure on the lyre I loved,
Their wholesome veins a-throb with life's strong flood,
Their finger tips a-glow with life's warm blood;
And as the notes grew sweet, and sweeter still,
Obedient to the promptings of my will,
What grewsome thought could my contentment bor-
Or whisper of the workings of a morrow?   [row,
Ah, well! to-day they sleep, the lyre is dumb,
Until some other restless touch shall come
To start its strings in wilder melody,
Till other tunes shall live, and fade. and die.

Farewell! No thought of thee am I to bear
Beyond this world of weakness and despair;
And yet I loathe thee not, as many say
Ethereal souls should loathe the mortal clay,
For thou wert given me my twin in birth ;
And though thou held'st me bounden unto earth
By thy delight in worldly luxury,
And that worst tie of human vanity,
Still I was sent to tame thy passions wild,
As loving mother governs wayward child.
Then when I failed, it was no sin of thine,
And when thou err'dst, it was through fault of mine.
Though all my earthly strife to thee I owe,
Though all life's bitterness thou didst bestow,
I loved thee well, the while thyself I wore,
And all thy frailties made me love thee more.
But fare-thee-well, cold image that thou art!
As Zenith and as Nadir far apart,
So are we twain henceforward, since to-day
Bids each of us forever take his way,
Thou, earthly-born, to earth eternally,
I upward. clothed in immortality.

TO BABY VIOLET.

When sunshine softened all the air of May,
There wandered in a flowered woodland way
A fair young mother, with her three small sons,
A-Maying. As the happy little ones
Gathered the purple violets with glee,
And ran to drop them at their mother's knee,
A gentle breeze that lingered in the air
To Heaven wafted her half-murmured prayer:
"Would violets might bloom the whole long year!"
The angels heard, and softly smiled to hear ;
And when at last the woodland flowers were gone,
There bloomed in a glad home, one lovely dawn,
A flower upon a tender mission bound—
One born to gladden hearts the whole year round,
The dearest, brightest, sweetest floweret—
A little human Baby Violet.

CHRISTMAS EVE.

When the cares of day were over at last.
   I put on my old, gray shawl
And started out in the lighted street,
   Repeating my errands all:

"There's the top I have promised to buy for Hal.
   And the new tin horse for Paul,
And my dear little Katie has set her heart
   On the painted, wooden doll."

The crowds of women were gaily dressed
   In gowns of the richest hues ;
The windows were all ablaze with light—
   I knew not where to choose.

At length I entered a gorgeous shop,
   And I paused, near the great glass door.
To gaze at a lovelier waxen doll
   Than I ever had seen before.

She could really open and shut her eyes!
   She wore a blue satin gown,
And I heard the man at the counter say
   'Twas the handsomest doll in town.

Then I thought of my wee little Kate at home,
  And oh, it was sin, I know !
But just for one moment I hated *my* lot,
  And I envied the rich folks so.

I stepped to the counter and asked to see
  Tin playthings—'twas hard to say,
Yes, hard to be sent back with the words :
  " Cheap toys are all down *that* way !"

It was then that I noticed a figure dark,
  A lady in black, near by ;
I felt that she saw, as I turned away,
  And I think she heard me sigh,

For when I had purchased my humble gifts
  And was going, I met her smile,
As touching me gently on the arm,
  She bade me to stop awhile.

And lo, she had bought a pair of skates,
  And a sled, and, oh, surprise !
The beautiful doll I'd been looking at,
  That could open and shut its eyes.

"Here, take them home to your hearth," she said ;
" In *my* home there'll be no light."
And she tried to stifle the sob that rose—
" 'Twas a year ago to-night."

Ah, I saw the drops in her sad, gray eyes,
  As over the toys she bent,
And my heart was so full that I could not speak.
  For I knew what the lady meant.

So now, if I'd only the cheap, tin toys
  And the plain little wooden doll,
My heart would be light on this Christmas eve,
  And beating with love for all.

For many's the heart, 'neath a thin-worn gown,
  That's brimming with gladness o'er,
And some of the saddest and heaviest hearts
  Roll by in a coach-and-four.

So I'll fill each dear little sock to-night,
  As my children lie fast asleep,
Then I'll wait for the sunshine to kiss their heads,
  As they rush to take their peep ;

And then, as they listen, I'll tell them there,
  Before they run off to play,
Of the little child-angel who sent these gifts
  To gladden their Christmas day.

HAYDN.

Quiet and peace fall gently over all,
As, eager, we await in breathless thrall
The wonderful awakening of the soul
That sleeps in silent harp, or written scroll.
It wakes ! First let the guiding spirit dwell
With soft adagio, then, for one charmed spell,
With quaint allegro, or with minuet.
Yes, nod your heads, ye venerable, let
Your hearts dance on, nor heed the warning voice
That feebly vetoes youth renewed ! Rejoice,
Ye happy young, unconscious, yet, of pain,
Let joy mount up and throb your every vein!
We'll steep our senses, quaff it deep to-night,
This draft of music, this quintessence bright.
Or, if again another change must be,
We'll back to tempo weird. If, momently,
Now sorrow's passion float upon the air,
We'll drift along, where'er the tide may bear;
Our hearts responsive vibrate to its pain,
Till it burst forth in rapturous song again,

With all the pleasure of existence stirred,
As, after storm, the weather-beaten bird
At the return of sunshine spreads its wings,
And joyous in the air, the while it sings,
Soars upward in its flight,
Heedless of coming night.

ON THE DEATH OF A YOUNG WOMAN.

(AFTER THE FRENCH OF DE MUSSET.)

Yes, she was kind, if it suffice
For kindness that she gave ; if free
Of hand may go with heart of ice—
If loveless alms be charity.

And she could pray—if handsome eyes,
Now downward bent with studied air,
Now upward lifted to the skies—
Be what we mortals mean by prayer.

She might have loved, if foolish pride,
Like this pale lamp now set apart
To light her body, had not spied
Upon her cold and barren heart.

Here in the gloom her coffin stands ;
She who has never lived is dead !
A book has fallen from her hands ;
Life's book—in which she has not read !

EVELYN.

On a hillside in the Grisons (sunny vale of Engadine)!
There's a church but newly builded, on whose spire a
    cross is seen,
And the evening service ended, and the priestly bless-
    ing given,
Out the people throng, and homeward turn to muse
    on life and Heaven.
In the sacred doorway lingering, knight and peasant
    maiden stand,
And the moon shines full upon them, as he stoops to
    press her hand.

From the church upon the hillside (joyful vale of
    Engadine)!
Bells are pealing, pealing madly. They are bridal
    bells, I ween ;
And the path is strewn with roses; all their perfume
    fills the air.
They are kneeling at the altar, knight and high-born
    lady fair.

From the church upon the hillside (mournful vale of
    Engadine)!
Bells are tolling, tolling sadly, funeral bells for Evelyn.
Now the nuns are chanting vespers, and the torches,
    burning low,
Light a girl's dead face, so beautiful, despite its trace
    of woe.

    *   *   *   *   *   *

On a hillside in the Grisons (sunny vale of Engadine)!
Stands a church time-worn and lonely, on whose spire
    a cross is seen,
And the traveler stops to wonder at its crumbling walls
    of stone,
Quaint old relic of the many centuries that are past
    and gone !

In the graveyard on the hillslope daisies spring and
    violets grow,
And the sun, forever smiling, sees them come—and
    sees them go.

KEATS.

There bloomed a plant of form and color fair,
But many men denied its beauty rare;
And as they passed it by, oh fate forlorn!
E'en laughed the sweetness of its breath to scorn.

One morn they woke to know full well its worth,
And came to place it in a richer earth,
Where it could feel the sunshine's warming light—
The shrinking plant had perished in the night!

FLOWERS FROM THE SHORES OF LAKE GENEVA.

Oh snowy, velvet edelweiss,
    The charm of Alpine height, its own
Pure spirit that 'mongst barren pines
    And jagged rocks blooms far alone!
Whence came you here, immortal child?
    From what high mountain came you down?

Say, did the fair-haired Switzer lad,
    From whose brown hand you first were mine,
Pursue the chamois' agile step,
    And thus your favorite haunt divine?
Howe'er it be, why here you lie
    To grace my flowers of Lang Syne.

Here's crocus pale from Jaman's side,
    And here's my brilliant gentian, too.
In cool retreat of mossy glade,
    There, wanderer, peeps the gentian's blue.
No other flower of mount or vale
    Can rival its celestial hue.

Here grasses grouped, from Chaudron's gorge,
  With Claren's violets are blent ;
Here clustered Alpine roses ; here
  Crisp ferns, whose earthy savor lent
Its essence to that isle enshrined
  Where rises Rousseau's monument.

This little, yellow primrose grew
  Apart, unknown to other flowers,
On one of those wee, tangled tufts,
  (Kept fresh and green through springtime showers)
With which, in patches here and there,
  Old Time has sodded Chillon's towers.

Perhaps, a hundred years ago,
  A sweet ancestral primrose sprung
Upon that self-same weedy tuft,
  And upward its faint odors flung
To where a little window pierced
  A gloomy vault, whence weak hands clung

To iron bars, and pale face peeped
  To catch a glimpse of Heaven's blue,
And heedless of the floweret's breath,
  The prisoner died, nor ever knew
That just without his dungeon wall
  A tiny, yellow primrose grew.

Dear, azure flower, to whose frail form
  My memories have clung so long !
This sweet forget-me-not has paled—
  Not so the slender, graceful throng
Which memory conjures fresh and blue—
  The sisters that she grew among.

Again I seem to see a quaint
  Old home, a vista wide of trees,
Beneath whose shade I wander forth,
  With all the joy of childhood's ease,
To gather the forget-me-nots
  That nod in soft midsummer breeze.

Sweet Lake Geneva ! though no more
  'Twere given me in idle hours
To roam your shores—your village walks,
  Your hills, your ivy-covered towers
No years can veil.   Your peaceful life
  I live again in these dear flowers.

A REMINISCENCE OF MUNICH.

In Munich is a well-known hall
Where the dead must wait ere their burial,
And a little girl, for coaxing rare,
Had begged till she was taken there.
She saw the dead, some young, some old,
Midst the costly flowers, lie white and cold,
In the stately pomp of a last display,
And her heart was awed, and she turned away.

Yet something lacked in this scene of death,
And she whispered softly, beneath her breath:
"But mother, where do they put the poor?"
Just then they saw, in a nook obscure,
A stooping creature, whose halting gait
Betrayed her age and her feeble state.
And the child went to her and asked, half shy:
"Will you tell me, please, where the poor folks lie?"

But she started back; for the woman's face
Seemed weird and frightful in such a place.
The poor old woman! she meant no harm,
But she grasped with fervor the little arm,

And frowning, and reaching out her head,
And pointing her bony finger, said:
" *There* lie the rich—and the poor *that way:*
But it's all the same for their souls to-day!"

I often think of that woman old,
Whose gesture wild, and whose sentence bold,
Prompted a child's first reasonings
On something deeper than childish things.
The years have glided, a hurrying throng.
She was so aged she must, since long
Have stretched her limbs where the poor folks lay—
But it's all the same for her soul to-day!

A DREAM OF THE SILENT RIVER.

I dreamed I wandered by a river;
Cold and deep that silent river !
From green banks of sunshine, yonder,
Lost in misty land of wonder,
Stretched a bridge from shore to shore.
Shadowy shapes were hurrying o'er.

As I gazed, my heart grew gloomy,
And a thrill of pain shot through me,
For amidst the throng's weird mazes
Oft I saw familiar faces ;
Swiftly, silently they moved—
Friends, companions I had loved—

Some with folded hands, resign'dly ;
Some, faint souls, uncertain, blindly ;
Some with hope, expectant, yearning ;
Some with many a backward turning,
And a little child I knew
Gave its hand and followed, too.

Said I: " Whither, phantoms, go ye ?
What lies behind yon mists, oh ! know ye?"
But never voice in answer lifted,
While helplessly their footsteps drifted
With the many, gone before,
And I saw their forms no more.

And to their unknown possession
Hurried on that dark procession,
Faster surging, onward ever,
O'er the deep, the silent river
Bound in death's resistless yoke—
And in sadness I awoke.

THE LITTLE SHEPHERD.

A little shepherd fell fast asleep
  On the bank of a rushing stream,
In the sunshine fair, and the sweet June air,
  And he had this curious dream :

He thought that he was a prince, and lived
  In a palace towering grand,
With wealth untold, and soldiers bold,
  All ready at his command.

And gay young lords with their ladies fair
  Were pacing the marble halls,
Where armour bright of many a knight
  Adorned the stately walls.

But all in the midst of his grandeur there,
  He listened, alas, in vain
For the welcome sound of a dear loved voice,
  And his pleasure turned to pain.

Just then a kiss fell on his cheek,
　And, raising his curly head,
In the deep blue skies of his mother's eyes
　He looked, and fondly said :

"Oh, not for all the castles gay,
　And not for a whole domain,
Were you not there my wealth to share,
　Would I be the prince again !"

THE SUN AND THE POPPIES.

Five little poppies opened their eyes,
One hazy dawn, to see the sun rise ;
And, as they looked, they said, each one :
" Oh, how I would like to be the sun ;
For it moves all round the world, so gay,
While we stand still in the field all day ! "

Five poppies watched the sun until
It faded and sank behind the hill ;
And they said : " After such a long trip about,
The poor old sun must be tired out ! "
And their drooping heads from the grass did peep,
And five little poppies fell fast asleep.

NATALIE.

By the Swannanoa river I rode; (ah, the night was
    chill!)
When the staring moon arose from behind a weird old
    mill;
And, keeping even pace.
We essayed a sudden race.
"Oh, moon, no maid serene
Awaits your kiss, I ween—
Why speed?" I cried in chaff—
But he looked a mocking laugh.

And along the river's brink I raced with the wild-
    faced moon,
Till we came on a spot where the air was rich from
    the locust's bloom,
Where the air was rich and sweet,
And my dear love watched to greet.
"Where'er your course may tend.
I have reached my journey's end,
Pale moon," I cried; "Adieu!"
Then I stopped—and the moon stopped, too.

Ah, lovely Natalie, how still in the air of June !
I bent to hide our fond embrace from the jealous moon.
But he touched her with his rays,
And I saw in his cold, wan rays,
My Natalie's white face,
My Natalie's dead face.
Then madly, in her sleep,
I bore her to the deep.

And oft, of a starlight night, we ascend from our
 watery rest ;
We float, and rise, and fall, with the Swannanoa's
 crest ;
We rise, and fall, and float,
To the Swannanoa's note,
Till the moon, with his haggard face,
Comes to gloat on her form of grace.
I seize her pale hand then
And we sink to the depths again.

BLEACHING.

(TO E. F. F.)

Oh, lightly swaying grasses
'Neath the linen soft and fair,
Bend your lithe forms with care,
As her graceful figure lingers,
And her little busy fingers
    Spread it there.

Oh, playful little zephyrs,
Do not blow it all away !
Let it bleach the livelong day,
So that, after all your kissing
Not a kerchief be found missing;
    Gently, pray !

Oh, glistening little sun rays,
Dancing on the grassy knoll,
On the linen, new and whole,
You may brighter shine, and brighter,
But you can not make it whiter
    Than her soul.

YESTERDAY AND TO-MORROW.

Two figures meet on the weary road
    Of life's dull every-day,
And, linking arm in arm, they walk
    Together the common way.

One is a child who is born of Hope,
    And, like Hope's children, bright;
Joy shines from her lifted azure eyes
    In liquid beams of light.

The other is robed in Sorrow's mist—
    She seems as a phantom wild—
And thus by day, as they journey far,
    She speaks to the spirit child:

"I once was a babe as fair as thou,
    With a gladness like to thine,
And wearied hearts sought promise sweet
    Of comfort at my shrine.

"But now my gifts are forgot by man,
    Who centers his thought in thee;
Or, if there linger my shadow dim,
    'Tis merged in thine imagery.

"My twilight fell when thy life to thee
  Its fairest promise gave.
Thy smiles, methinks, are like budding flowers
  That spring from a new-made grave."

Then sweetly, sadly, the child of Hope
  Low murmurs: "Ah me! ah me!
My time is brief, for what thou art,
  My sister, I soon shall be."

And they twine their arms in a firmer clasp,
  Along on the common way,
And forth with the years they slowly glide,
  To-Morrow and Yesterday.